First Edition 2019

ISBN 978-0-9990249-7-3
Library of Congress Control Number 2019930212
2 4 6 8 10 9 7 5 3 1
Printed in China

Creative Director: Robert Broder
This book was typeset in Geneva.
The illustrations were rendered in a combination of traditional mixed media
techniques (acrylics and oil colors and colored pencils) and digital detailing.

Ripple Grove
Press
Shelburne, Vermont
RippleGrovePress.com

Thank you for reading.

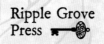

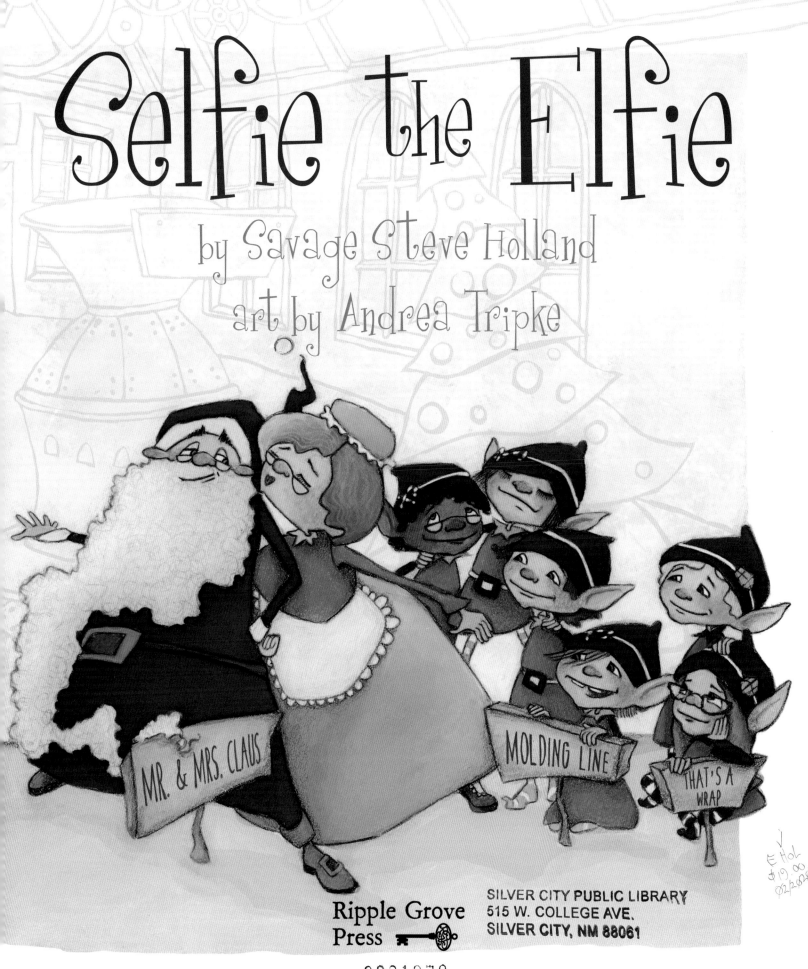

Selfie the Elfie

by Savage Steve Holland

art by Andrea Tripke

Ripple Grove Press 🔑

Way up north,
in a place so cold, even the polar bears wear ugly sweaters,
sits the busiest,
happiest,
most magical place of all . . .
Santa's workshop!

R & D

TOY TESTER

Molding Line

Wish Lists

In Santa's workshop
all the elves were busy
building,
gluing,
and preparing for the
most special day of the year . . .
Christmas!

But there was one elf in Santa's workshop who had a talent with ribbon.

Her name was . . . **Sophie!**

Sophie was in charge of tying bows on every present
that was stuffed into Santa's sleigh.

She could tie
any kind of bow:
big or small,
fancy or plain.

She could create layered loops and figure eights,
bunny ears and donkey tails!

Sophie was so proud of her bows, she snapped pictures of them with her handy-dandy camera phone.

Eventually, Sophie was not only taking pictures of her bows—
she started taking pictures of . . . **herself!**

Sophie took so many selfies
that soon the other elves got
sidetracked from their jobs.

They tried to ignore
Sophie's selfies,
but it was difficult.

She just had to take a selfie with the North Pole Snowman Choir.

But asking them to come inside was not the best idea.

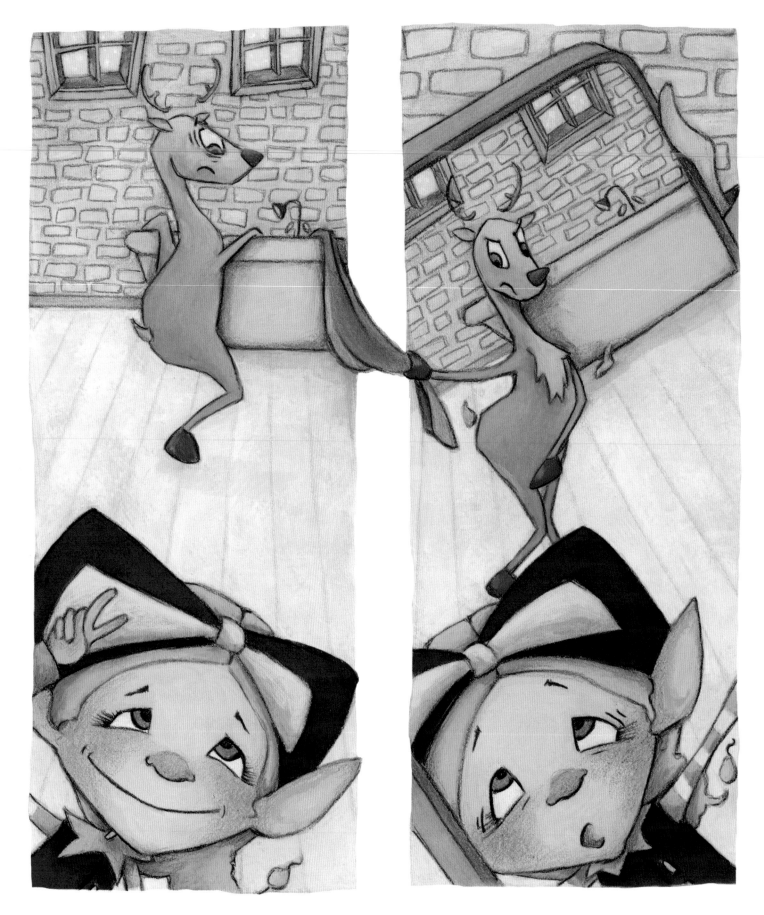

Sophie snapped an awkward selfie with a reindeer.
But even reindeer need privacy.

She snuck in on Santa,
who was trying to enjoy some quiet time.

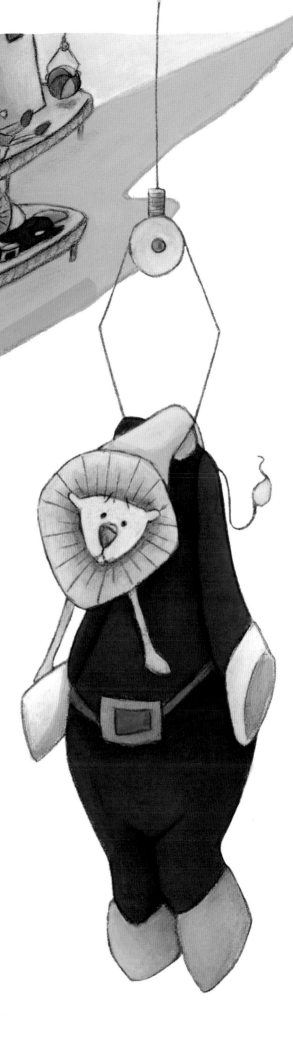

When Mrs. Claus brought out
Santa's legendary,
one-and-only,
Big Night Delivery Suit,

Sophie just had to have a selfie!

Sophie was so busy taking selfies that she fell behind on her work.

When Santa came to check on Christmas Eve preparations,
he noticed piles of presents without any bows.
With a twinkle in his eye, Santa bellowed, "Sophie!"

She sprinted back to her ribbons before you could say, "Nutcracker."

With a twist and a tie and a loop and a swoop, Sophie was all caught up.

But she couldn't resist taking more pictures of her bows and of . . . **herself!**

She posed with the elves at the toy-making station,
who were easily distracted.

Sophie was a bit naughty and a bit nice snapping a selfie with the top-secret list.

She stood in front of the workshop's Christmas tree. The reflections in the ornaments let Sophie take a selfie of herself taking a selfie.

At last, it was time for Christmas.

The sleigh was ready.
The reindeer were ready.
The presents were ready, bows and all.

But when Santa walked
into the workshop,
Santa wasn't ready!

"Where's my suit?" he cried.

The elves searched high and low. No suit in sight.
The reindeer looked outside. No suit in sight.

Even the polar bears peeked in their closets.
No. Suit. In. Sight.

"Sophie!" called Mrs. Claus. "Can you please put down the phone?
We could really use your help!"

But something in the selfies caught Sophie's eye.

"Holy eggnog!" she yelled.
"Here it is!"

Everyone was overjoyed
and relieved!

"Sophie! Or shall I call you
Selfie the Elfie?!" Santa cheered.
"Your selfies saved Christmas!"

Santa quickly put on his suit
and boarded his sleigh.

He clicked to the reindeer,
and he was off with a jolly . . .

The next day, after the work was done, all the toys were delivered,

and Santa was home safe and warm,

Sophie gathered everyone
in the workshop for a selfie.
They all shouted out with glee,
Merry Christmas!

To Clementine, Ottoli, Zuzu, Cajun, and my own Saint NiColle.
You fill my workshop with laughter. —S.S.H.

For Maja and Jona. —A.T.